← Crumpler is extremely shy.

Pootle and Poppet can → be very silly sometimes...

Gibbet hates knotted string.

Nik-Nak is afraid of chickens.

To Mum, thank you for cardboard cars and sandwiches - M.B.

For Mum and Dad, the big ones and the little ones, Grandma and
Grandpa, Aunty Lynden and dear Grandpa Arthur.
Thank you for believing in me. xx - S.A.

A TEMPLAR BOOK

First published in the UK in 2011 by Templar Publishing,
an imprint of The Templar Company Limited,
The Granary, North Street, Dorking, Surrey, RH4 1DN, UK
www.templarco.co.uk

First edition

ISBN 978-1-84877-204-5

Designed by Leonard Le Rolland and Manhar Chauhan
Edited by Emma Goldhawk

Printed in China

HECTOR

Mark Barry

illustrated by Sarah Aspinall

templar publishing

Hector was a dreamer.

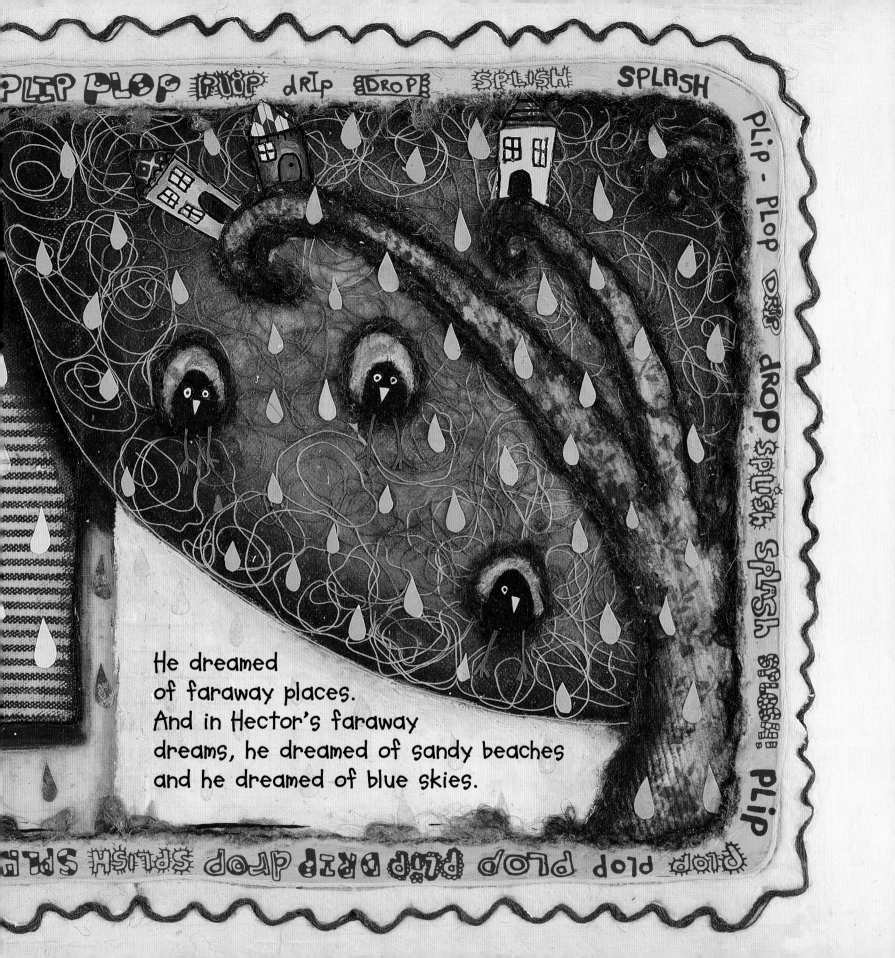

PLIP PLOP PLIP dRIP dROP SPLISH SPLASH

He dreamed
of faraway places.
And in Hector's faraway
dreams, he dreamed of sandy beaches
and he dreamed of blue skies.

Hector got out his best colouring
pencils and paints and dreamed up
a picture of a big, bright-red car.

Then he stuck the picture on the wall.

A little while later,
Hector's friends, Pootle
and Poppet, arrived.
Hector showed them
his new picture.

"What's that?" said Pootle.
"My big, bright-red car," said Hector. "It's going
to take me to faraway places."
"But you don't have a big, bright-red car," said Poppet.
"I know," said Hector.
"Shall we help you to build it?" said Pootle.
"That would be nice," said Hector.

SQUIGGLE

Herbert

Bob

STAMP

SURPRISE

HECTOR!

CrUmPlER

I ♥ CARS

Gibbet

POOTLE and

POPPET

NIK - NAK

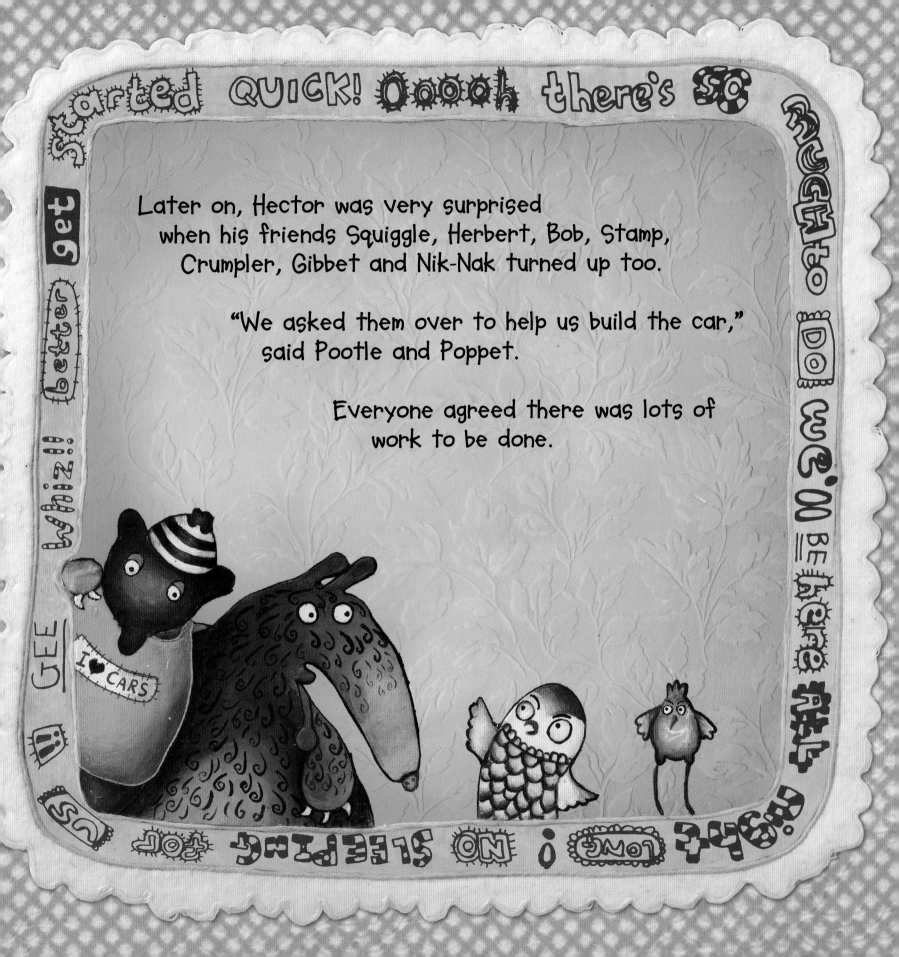

Later on, Hector was very surprised
when his friends Squiggle, Herbert, Bob, Stamp,
Crumpler, Gibbet and Nik-Nak turned up too.

"We asked them over to help us build the car,"
said Pootle and Poppet.

Everyone agreed there was lots of
work to be done.

Nik-Nak, Stamp, Gibbet and Crumpler cut cardboard. Squiggle, Herbert and Bob glued. Pootle and Poppet taped, and...

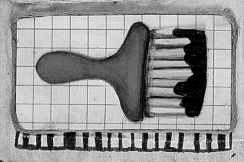

Hector made lots and lots and lots of sandwiches.

After a lot of hard work, the car was almost ready. Hector fixed the last wheel in place. Nik-Nak, Stamp, Gibbet, Crumpler, Squiggle, Herbert and Bob all agreed the big, bright-red car was brilliant.

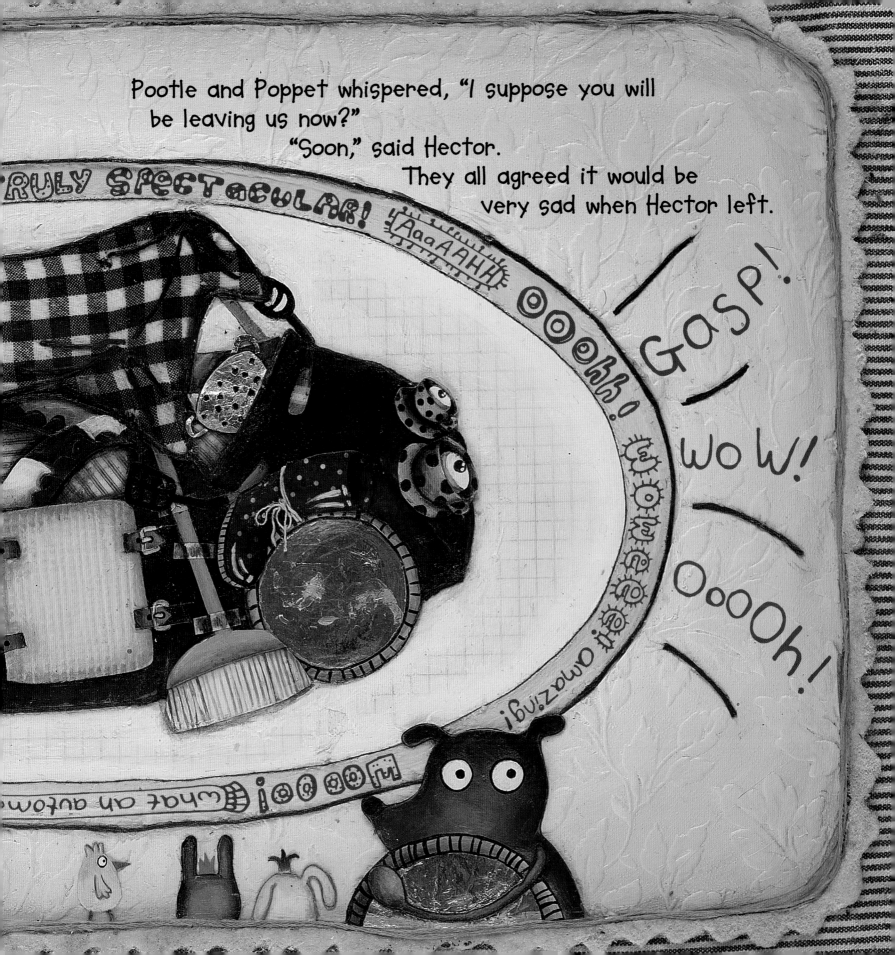

Pootle and Poppet whispered, "I suppose you will be leaving us now?"

"Soon," said Hector.

They all agreed it would be very sad when Hector left.

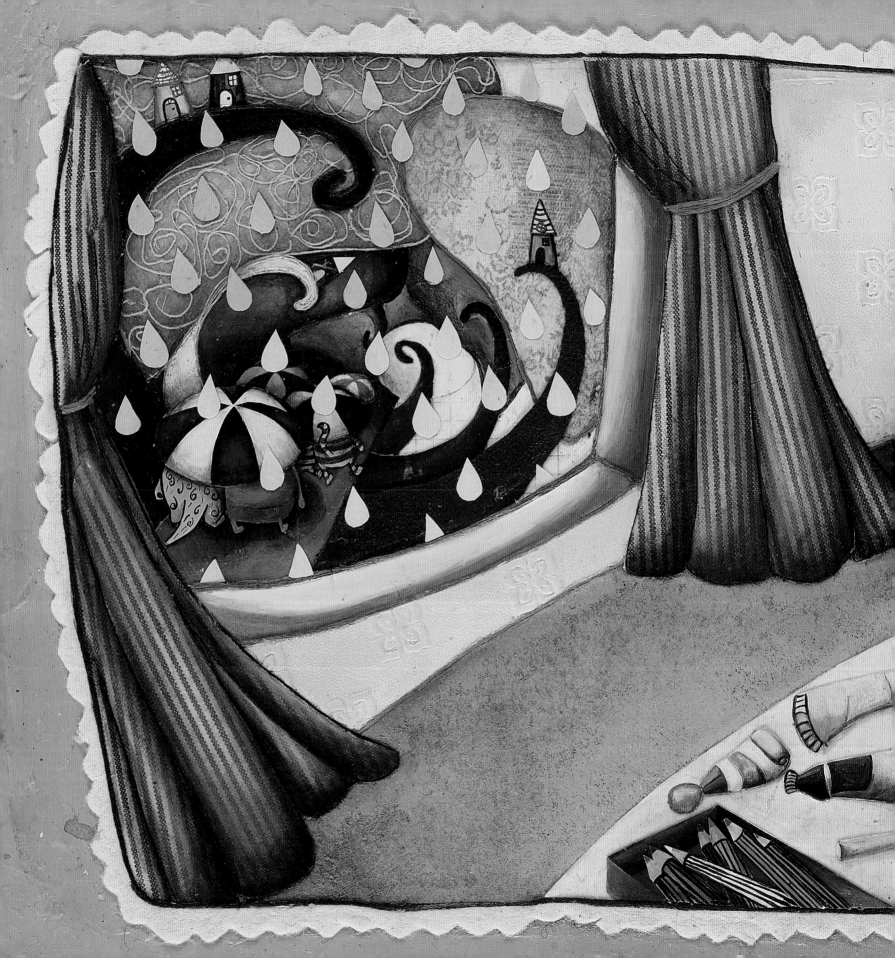

Later, when his friends had gone, Hector got out his best colouring pencils and paints again and dreamed up a picture of some trees.

some clouds floating by...

a big yellow sun...

and a seaside.

Finally, the day came for Hector to go. Nik-Nak, Stamp, Gibbet, Crumpler, Squiggle, Herbert, Bob, Pootle and Poppet all came to see him off in his big, bright-red car.

"You've made a lot of sandwiches," said Crumpler.
"I know," said Hector.
"A lot for just one Hector," said Herbert.
"I know," said Hector.
"Shall we all come too?" said Pootle
and Poppet.

"No faraway place
would be any fun
without my friends,"
said Hector.

So they all pushed the bright-red car until they reached a faraway place with trees and houses, and little shops, and a big blue sky, and floating clouds, and a big yellow sun.

Then they all had fun together
at the seaside of Hector's dreams.
And Hector? Well, he was thinking about where
his paints and pencils might take them next.

so does Herbert.

Bob likes hats....

Squiggle sleeps on a whoopie cushion.

Stamp always gets too close to the camera.